Tom and Pippo's Day

PIPPO

HELEN OXENBURY

ALADDIN BOOKS
Macmillan Publishing Company • New York

When I wake up early in the
morning, first I give Pippo a hug.

Then we go to see if Mommy
and Daddy are awake.

Daddy has to
hurry with
his breakfast.
Sometimes I give Pippo some of
mine, but he's so clumsy and
he makes a mess.

Pippo and I do things together all day, until Daddy comes home.

When it's bedtime, sometimes I
don't know where Pippo is and
I have to look everywhere
until I find him.

Because when it's time
to go to sleep,
I need to be
with Pippo.